It's fun to go to school

J. B. Lippincott
New York

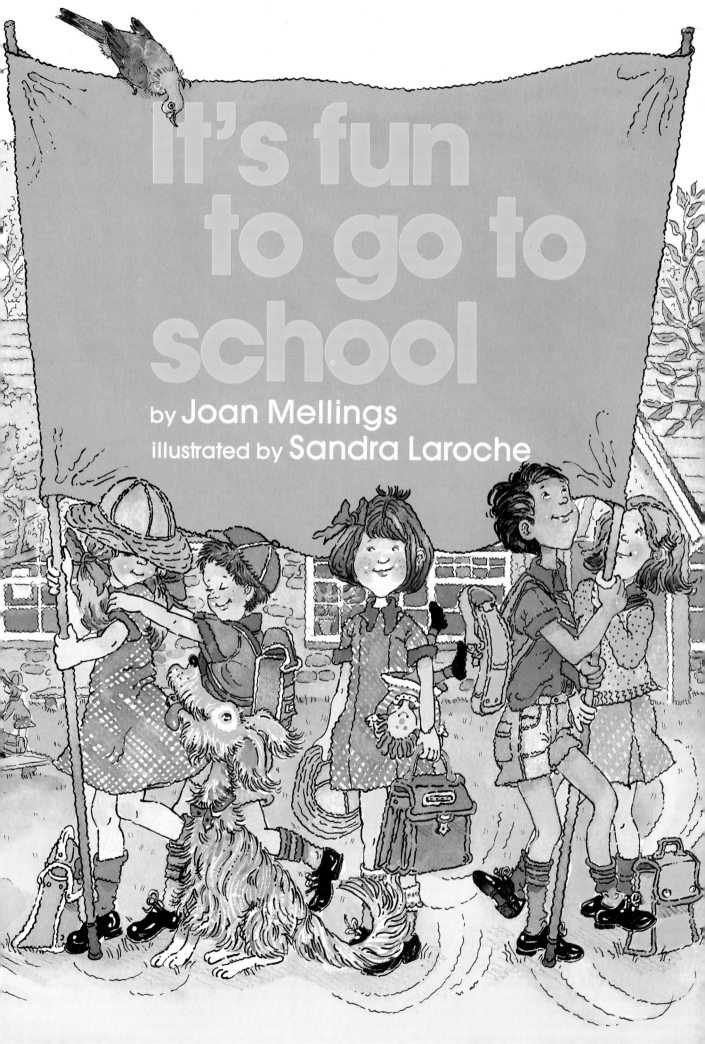

It's fun to go to school

by Joan Mellings

illustrated by Sandra Laroche

We've been to the stores
It was such fun to choose

School bags and crayons,
Clothes and shoes.

I'm going to school,
Now that I'm five.
I've waited so long
For this day to arrive.

I have a friend,
Virginia Sue.
She's five, and is ready
To go to school too.

In through the school gate,
Faces all around,

Wide open doorway,
New, happy sound.

At school I have a locker
My books and lunch are there,
A little, private place for me,
The only thing that I don't share.

Pegs on the wall
To hang coats and hats,
Into the classroom
To sit on bright mats.

The classroom is big and the windows are wide,
It makes me feel sometimes that I'm still outside.

On the walls there are pictures
Of so many things –
Boats, trees and animals,
Castles and kings.

On our first day at school
We are all shown around

The library and bathroom
And the big playground.

Our teacher is friendly,
And she knows all our names.
She tells exciting stories
And joins in all our games.

Sometimes our teacher makes a game
Of things we have to do.
She says "Now let us all be cows,
Moo — Moo — Moo!"

When I want to go to the bathroom,
I let the teacher know.
I raise my hand up in the air,
She always lets me go.

And afterwards I wash my hands,
Sometimes I wash my face,
Then run back to the classroom
And sit down in my place.

Cross the road carefully,
Look left and right.

Don't take a step
Till you see the green light.

It's wet today! It's wet today!
But I don't want to stay away.

My yellow raincoat keeps me dry
When rain is falling from the sky.

A part of each day
We dance and we sing.
We all choose a partner
And skip in a ring.

Today we had rhythm,
I beat the drum.
The others played tambourines,
Rum — tum — tum.

Sit very still,
Work is all done,
Soon we'll go home
But school is such fun!

At night when I'm in bed,
I think about the day
And all the things I did at school,
To learn to work and play.

It's Fun to Go to School

First published in England by Hamlyn Publishing,
Twickenham, Middlesex.

Copyright © 1985 by Lansdowne Press

All rights reserved. Printed in South Korea.
For information address Harper & Row Junior Books,
10 East 53rd Street, New York, N.Y. 10022.
First American Edition.

Library of Congress Catalog Number 85-45771
ISBN 0-694-00125-2